EMBRACING SHADOW

Ruby's Journey

Embracing Shadow

Ruby's Journey

Alina V. Shi

For you, the reader:

May Ruby's journey gently remind you
that courage often begins quietly.

Contents

Author's Note

Embracing Shadow weaves a fictional tale that nevertheless reveals my fascination with personal narratives of growth and healing. The people, the moments, and the places in this book all came from my imagination — but what they carry is real to me: family, friendship.

It's the grit to keep moving, and the courage to step forward when every part of you wants to stay still. You find it in little moments — a decision made in silence, a choice no one notices — and I wanted Ruby's world to be made of those moments too.

Chapter 1

A Shattered Past

*W*ant to hang out?

Aqua's text shone from her phone screen like a mocking memory of happier times. Her best friend had been asking her to hang out for days. Normally, Ruby would love to. But lately...

shadows seemed to lurk in her mind. And voices. But those she pushed away.

Ruby ignored the text and turned up her music. Aqua had a great life, and she didn't want to tell her best friend all the ways her own life was... shattered.

Ruby sat still in her worn, comfortable armchair and looked out her bedroom window. The sun had set over the sea, sending up a bright array of pink, purple, red, orange, and yellow. She loved the way the colors melted into one indescribably magnificent hue. The fading light made the clouds look ethereal.

The sight would have taken her breath away just a few years ago. But now, like so many things that used to bring her joy, it served as a reminder of what she had lost.

Soon, the sky turned dark, and Ruby shrugged; she hated sunsets, anyway.

Music from her phone was sending gentle, calm vibes through her earbuds... until it stopped abruptly. She tensed in her chair. The music was replaced by screams, cries, and wails.

This was what her life had come to. And she hated it.

The jarring transition from calm to chaos, from escape to reality made her flinch. She felt anxious. Alone. Isolated. Her fingers fumbled with her phone, trying to restore the calming music, bring back that sacred shield against everything that was wrong in her life. But before she could fix it—

"Ruby, get down here!" her mother screamed.

"I can't," Ruby whispered. But she had to. She was only fifteen, and her mom could still tell her what to do.

The shrill command cut through the air, making Ruby's shoulders hike up to her ears. She recognized that tone—it meant her mother had been drinking again. Whatever peace Ruby had found in her solitude was about to be shattered.

With a groan, Ruby slowly got out of her chair, pulled out her earbuds, and trudged downstairs. Each step felt like a countdown to another angry confrontation, another moment where she would have to be the adult, another reminder that this house had lost its foundation.

She barely noticed the old and faded framed pictures of her family along the wall on the way down, except for one—a picture of her father standing next to her older brother, both smiling. She stopped in her tracks. She missed them so much that it caused pains in her chest. She couldn't stand *not having them around* any longer. It had been five years since that fateful Greyhound bus trip. Her father was sending her brother off to college. Somewhere just outside of Chicago, a suburb where nothing grew but pine trees, and dried needles covered the ground like nature's own carpeting.

The photograph captured a moment frozen in time—her father's eyes crinkling at the corners in that way they always did when he was truly happy, Liam's smile wide and unguarded as they stood together in front of their house. They wore matching plaid shirts, something Ruby had teased them about.

"You two look like lumberjacks," she had said, and Liam had chased her around the yard while their father laughed, deep and warm.

That laughter still echoed in her memories, a sound she desperately tried to hold onto even as it seemed to fade a little more each passing year. The photo had been taken just days before they left, before everything changed, before their family was torn apart by a tragedy that none of them saw coming.

Even as her mother's voice shouted at her again, she clung to the memory of the two people she needed most. Their smiles reminded her of how things might have been, rather than what they had become.

The sound of glass clinking from the kitchen below pulled her back to the present moment. Her mother would be waiting, probably with another empty bottle beside her, ready to unleash whatever frustrations had built up throughout the day. Ruby took a deep breath, steeling herself for what was to come. She had learned to read the signs—the tone of her mother's voice, the time of day she started calling, the sharp edge to her words that signaled she'd been drinking again.

Knowing her mother was likely just about to scream for her again, Ruby hustled down the last few steps.

You're doing it again... hiding. The voice hissed outside her brain, somewhere from the air around her.

Ruby clenched her teeth. The voice came and went, never accompanied by a face but always sending a rush of anger and fire through her.

"Not now," she muttered to nothing.

She had to worry about her mom, not some voice she kept hearing. With her mom, it was better to just do what she wanted and avoid the consequences of her mom's anger. Ruby landed at the bottom of the stairs with a thump. The old floorboard creaked beneath her feet, announcing her arrival like an unwanted herald.

Rounding the corner into the kitchen, Ruby was met with the sickening, acidic smell of alcohol that seemed to have become as much a part of their house as the paint on the walls. Her mom never drank when her dad was still alive.

Ruby sighed—it looked like her mother had been drinking more than usual. The realization sat heavy in Ruby's stomach as she took in the scene before her.

"Ruby! Explain this!" her mother slurred. She waved a phone wildly as she pointed at Ruby's sister Mia, who was wailing at the kitchen table. Her eyes glassy, she staggered slightly, voice trembling with fury.

"I don't know, Mom," Ruby replied, her voice tight, emotionless.

"I'm not your mother," she snapped back crazily. Her voice echoed off the chipped tile like it didn't quite belong in the room.

The words hung in the air like smoke, and even her mother seemed momentarily surprised by them. She blinked, swayed slightly, and looked down at her glass, as if trying to remember how much she had actually drunk.

Her gaze flicked to Mia, then back to Ruby. For a moment—just a flicker—something softened. Regret? Fear? But then her face hardened again, and she straightened her back like a marionette tugged by pride.

Trying to deflect the dull ache her mother's words could still inflict, Ruby's face turned expressionless. Emotion just made everything worse. "I swear I didn't touch that brat's phone!" she hissed.

Mia's wailing only got louder, but Ruby could see through her sister's act. She was doing this just to get Ruby in trouble.

Her mom, now furious, said, "I'm so done with you, Ruby. All you do is cause trouble. *You're moving out tomorrow and going to live with your grandma.* Now go, pack!"

Ruby chose not to react, not to give either of them the satisfaction of believing they had hurt her. Wordlessly, she shot one last glance at her mother then her sister, who gave her a smug smile. Tomorrow, would her mom even remember this threat? Ruby stormed back upstairs, slammed her door shut, and stood in the silence of her room, her chest heaving with a mix of relief and the pain that marked every day of her life in that house.

For a long moment, she didn't move.

The familiar walls seemed to close in on her, pressing against the ache in her chest. The posters, the childhood trophies, the glow-in-the-dark stars she had stuck to the ceiling when she was nine—they all felt like echoes from a different life. Her eyes caught the corner of a framed photo of her brother Liam, tucked half-behind her bookshelf.

She pressed her forehead to the door, willing the tears not to come. Her hands were still clenched into fists. She wasn't even sixteen, but she felt eighty from the weight she was carrying.

"I can't do this anymore," she whispered, barely audible. Her voice shook, and she hated how small she felt.

Crossing the room, she caught her reflection in the mirror. Her face looked unfamiliar—red from anger, shadows under her eyes, her expression so much older than it should have been.

It wasn't fair. None of it.

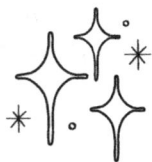

Chapter 2

Dad and Liam

S he walked to the bed like her body
had given up fighting, and when
she dropped onto the mattress, it wasn't
just from exhaustion—it was surren-
der.

Shadow jumped onto the bed next
to her, purring softly as he curled up

close to Ruby's side. He made his presence known by rubbing his nose into Ruby's hand. Ruby stroked Shadow's fur, and this gave them both a little measure of comfort.

Before she could close her eyes, the smiling picture of her dad and brother from the wall flashed through her mind. Along with it, memories of a happier time. Before trauma hit their family hard.

She could picture the scene as if it was just now happening...

The scent of pine needles and sea salt lingered in the cool morning air as Ruby scrambled up a rocky outcrop, her sneakers slipping slightly on the uneven surface. She was eleven then. Her laughter echoed through the forest as pure and clear as a bell. Below her, her father steadied her with a firm hand while Liam climbed effortlessly beside her, his long legs making the task look easy.

"Slow down, Speedy," her dad called, his deep voice tinged with amusement and that ever-present note of protective care. "Not all of us are mountain goats."

"I'm not a goat!" Ruby called back, grinning as she reached the top, the wind whipping her hair around her face. "I'm a bird!"

She spread her arms wide, pretending to soar above the world, above all its troubles and sorrows. Liam reached her a moment later, his breath steady despite the climb, his presence as solid and reassuring as the rocks beneath their feet. "More like a penguin," he teased, ruffling her hair in that annoying-but-loving way only big brothers could have.

"Hey!" Ruby protested, swatting his hand away. But she couldn't keep the smile from her face.

Their father joined them at the summit, laughing as he placed an arm around each of their shoulders. His presence was like a shield against the world, strong and unwavering. "Alright, you two. Truce. We're here to enjoy the view, not start a wrestling match."

Ruby huffed but quickly forgot her annoyance as she looked out over the sparkling expanse of the ocean. The waves crashed rhythmically against the cliffs below, their sound soothing and endless, a natural symphony that seemed to speak directly to her soul. The vastness of the sea stretched before them, meeting the horizon in a seamless blend of blues that made it impossible to tell where ocean ended and sky began.

"This is my favorite spot," she declared, leaning into her dad's side, drawing comfort from his solid presence. "It's perfect."

"It is," he agreed, squeezing her

gently. His voice carried that special warmth reserved just for his children. "And you know what makes it even better?"

"What?" Ruby asked, looking up at him expectantly, her eyes wide with curiosity and trust.

"Sharing it with you two," he said, his voice warm and full of love that seemed to wrap around them like a blanket. "You're my greatest treasures, you know that?"

Ruby giggled at that, and Liam rolled his eyes, though a smile tugged at his lips. "Come on, Dad, you're getting all sappy," Liam protested, but he didn't move away from their father's embrace.

"Let me be sappy," their dad replied, his tone mock serious though his eyes twinkled with joy. *"One day, you'll understand."*

The memory faded like the tide pulling away from the shore, leaving Ruby alone in a house that felt too cold, too cruel to really be hers. Her father's words echoed in her mind with painful clarity: One day, you'll understand.

She did understand now—too well.

Her dad and Liam had been her anchors, their steady presence keeping her world balanced. Without them, she felt like a ship adrift in stormy seas, searching for a lighthouse that no longer shone. Ruby blinked back tears, her chest tightening with an ache that had become all too familiar.

The pain of their absence was a constant weight, but in moments like this, when memories surfaced with such vivid clarity, it felt almost unbearable.

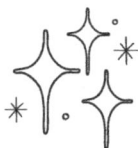

Chapter 3

Shadow and Shelter

M oving like a ghost, the black cat peered into Ruby's eyes. For an instant she felt like he knew exactly what she was going through. As he sat close to her, she could feel the warmth enveloping her, and slowly he began to purr. The soothing sound vibrated the bed, and slowly and gently, her heart began to heal.

Three months after the incident that took her dad and brother she'd spotted Shadow in the backyard. Although, it almost felt *that he spotted her.* She was sitting on the fence trying to hide from one of her mother's verbal attacks when she saw him. Shadow had jumped up on the fence next to her, looking at her in that deep way that cats have. She knew they'd be inseparable from that moment. And they had been.

"At least, you are here," she muttered under her breath, barely able to be heard over his purring. Shadow was pushed in even closer, and the sound of his purring grew louder—as if he was there to tell her that he was not going anywhere. This was their ritual.

They had created it after a series of long, tough nights when the house was too much and the memories were too loud.

Instead of packing as her mother had demanded, Ruby convinced herself that her mom was just drunk and didn't mean what she had said. Emotionally exhausted from all the drama, she soon fell asleep, Shadow's steady presence anchoring her to reality even as her mind began to drift far away from it in sleep.

Chapter 4

Sapphire City

W hat felt like only a moment later, Ruby awoke to find herself in a totally different room basking in warm sunlight. She felt her worries fade. Her eyes took in her surroundings. Instinctively, she knew this place. Sapphire City, the city of emotions.

The only piece of furniture was a bed beneath a large window that looked out onto an incredible sight: futuristic flying cars, gleaming sky-scrapers that dwarfed the clouds behind them, dazzling light displays, and robotic street vendors everywhere. However, the traffic was loud, and people were shouting at one another. It wasn't heaven on earth as she had first imagined it might be.

In fact, it was more like hell.

The city pulsed with an energy that felt somehow connected to her own emotional turbulence. Each flash of light, each mechanical whir, each shout from below seemed to echo something inside her—the anger, the grief, the confusion she'd been trying so hard to suppress. Was there no escape from her feelings?

Intrigued by everything she was

seeing, Ruby stepped out of the room and onto the glass streets.

On an enormous screen flashed the face of a girl who looked just like her: sun-kissed skin with a sprinkle of freckles across her nose, bright hazel eyes framed by naturally full lashes, and lips curved into a tentative smile, all encased by wayward strands of sun-bleached hair that had escaped her messy ponytail.

"Hello, Emotion members," the girl said. "I'm Sapphire, and I'm here to make this world spin." Ruby was baffled, not only was there an imposter of her—but just what, why, *and how* was any of this happening?

As a young girl, Ruby had always dreamed of cities full of wonders like this one. But that spark of imagination had all but dwindled after her dad and brother had perished. Suddenly, she saw a girl and an old man fighting across the street.

Both concerned and curious, Ruby approached them and immediately had to do a double take—*the girl looked exactly like Aqua*, Ruby's best friend.

"Hey," the girl yelled out to her. "Hey, you! Help me finish this guy off here, will you? He took my money."

Ruby was perplexed and sent the combative girl a look of uncertainty. When Ruby didn't do what the girl wanted, the girl's face turned to pure rage. She became like a jackhammer, pounding the man across the face over again until the stolen cash fell out of his back pocket. Frozen in place, Ruby was terrified by the intensity of the girl's anger.

The girl retrieved the wad of money and was about to leave when Ruby ventured to call out. Her curiosity having overpowered her fear. "Aqua?"

The girl scoffed. "Who? Inferno's my name," she spit out. Ruby knew that voice; she'd heard it too many times to count inside her own mind when she was awake. Puffing her chest out, Inferno marched over to Ruby.

Inferno's eyes widened when she got a closer look at Ruby. "Oh, forgive me, Lady Sapphire! I am so sorry!"

Confused, Ruby had no idea what she was talking about. Seeing this girl named Inferno profusely apologizing over giving her attitude, Ruby knew something was off. "No, no, no. I'm not Sapphire, but can you help me?"

Ruby explained to Inferno how she had arrived and about the look-alikes in this world and hers.

"Huh, well, I don't know much but I do know this: Lady Sapphire created each of us and she lives in that tower over there." Inferno gestured toward a tall gray castle with two towers spiraling high into the sky, as if Ruby couldn't see it otherwise. "It seems like everything's falling apart lately because *everyone has lost control of their feelings.*"

"Whoa," Ruby cried out as a loud crackle from below interrupted them. The ground started shaking. Ruby's sneakers skidded on cracking glass. The bridge groaned like it was tired of holding itself together—*join the club.*

"You're the architect here," Sapphire called from a floating billboard.

Her blue hair whipped sideways, but the rest of her stayed perfectly still. Creepy, like a glitching video game character.

"I didn't build this!" Ruby grabbed a lamppost. The metal burned her palm.

Or maybe that was her own salty sweat.

Sapphire leapt down, landing in a crouch. Up close, her eyes weren't blue like Ruby expected—more gray, like Dad's old hoodie after too many washes. "Every time you swallow a memory or deny an emotion, the city eats itself."

The ground lurched. Ruby's stomach flipped. *Fifth grade rollercoaster, Liam's hand squeezing her—*

"Stop!" Sapphire yanked her upright. "Feed the city truth or it'll feed on you."

Ruby spat out the first thing that hurt: "I didn't say goodbye at the station. I was mad about stupid—*stupid—*"

The cracks slowed. The bridge held.

Sapphire nodded. "Now you're speaking its language."

The city shattered—

—and Ruby woke with a gasp, burnt sugar thick on her tongue. Salt-water soaked the sheets. Not sweat. Not tears. *The ocean.* Dad's ocean, the one that seeped into everything.

She scrubbed her hands against her jeans. Glass dust glittered in the moon-light, real as the clock's glare: 3:17 a.m. Always 3:17.

Shadow butted his head against her wrist. *Real.* The cat's fur smelled like home, not ozone. No skyscrapers. No screaming streets. Just her tasteless room and the weight of her mother's voice, frayed at the edges like a bad radio signal.

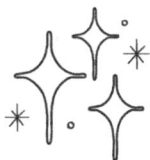

Chapter 5

Alex

Ruby's phone buzzed with a text from Aqua: *Hey, you up? Need to talk.*

Ruby stared at the message, her fingers hovering over the keyboard. Aqua had been her best friend since fifth grade when they'd bonded over their shared love of basketball and their equally terrible attempts at art class. Back then, everything had been simpler. They could talk about anything—boys, movies, jokes—staying up late trading secrets and giggling until their sides hurt. But that was before the accident.

Just tired. Talk tomorrow? Ruby typed back, then immediately felt guilty for ignoring so many messages and then dodging other ones. This was becoming a pattern—Aqua reaching out, Ruby pulling away.

Her phone buzzed again. *You've been saying that a lot lately. Everything ok?*

Ruby's chest tightened. How could she explain what was happening when she barely understood it herself? How could she tell Aqua about seeing her lookalike, Inferno, in that strange dream city? The old Ruby would have already called Aqua, would have spilled everything. But now...

Yeah, just stressed about the history test, Ruby replied, adding a casual "☺" to mask the lie.

There was a long pause before Aqua's response came through: *Ok. You know you can tell me anything, right?*

Ruby stared at those words until her vision blurred. *I know,* she texted back, but her throat felt tight with unspoken truths.

She dressed quickly, snagged her backpack, and headed out of her bedroom.

When she got downstairs, her mom was slouched over the kitchen table with an empty wine bottle beside her. Her little sister Mia sat quietly directly across the table, eating cereal and watching Ruby with the large and curious eyes of a cat wondering if they had pushed their caregiver too far.

"Are you leaving?" Mia finally broke the silence with a concerned whisper.

Ruby sighed and ruffled Mia's hair. "I don't know, kiddo. I guess we'll see."

Mia looked relieved and went back to her cereal. Shadow rubbed against Ruby's legs, and she bent down to scratch behind the cat's ears. She left for school and the cool morning air was a welcome relief from the night's heated events. She walked to school lost in thoughts about Sapphire City and Inferno. *What did it all mean? Am I losing my mind?*

She saw Alex waiting for her in the courtyard where all the seniors hung out. Alex was a tall, lean boy with messy light brown hair and bright blue eyes, dressed casually in a gray hoodie and jeans. They had been close friends since fifth grade. He waved her over and noticed immediately that something was wrong. With concern etched on his face, he asked, "Hey, are you ok?"

Ruby forced a smile, glad to see him. "Yeah, I just had a weird dream."

"Wanna talk about it?"

Ruby hesitated but then nodded. "There was this city. All glass and metal and chaos. And there was this girl who looked just like me, but with blue hair. She said..." Ruby paused, gathering her thoughts. "She said I was causing the chaos because I wouldn't deal with my emotions."

Alex nodded thoughtfully. "Maybe she has a point."

Ruby started to protest, but the words died in her throat. Last night's dream flashed through her mind again—the twisting buildings, the stormy skies, all of it reflecting her inner turmoil. "Maybe," she conceded. "But I don't know how to deal with any of it."

"You know," Alex said carefully, "I started seeing Dr. Matthews after my grandmother died. It... it helped. More than I thought it would."

"Helped how?" Ruby asked cautiously.

"All I could think about after I lost her was how unfair it was."

Ruby nodded, but Alex shook his head. "No, how unfair it was that it was beautiful outside at her funeral. How... normal everything else was for everyone else. But not for me. I wanted everyone to cry or pitch a fit, maybe." He shrugged. "Just for them to show that they hated death as much as me. Missed her the way I did."

Ruby understood.

"I... I had nightmares. Not right away. Grief goes in cycles, you know. I dreamed about a cold kitchen, an empty chair, a voice calling my name from behind a closed door. I would wake up sweating, heart racing, convinced she was just on the other side—only to be met by silence."

"How did you make it all stop?" Ruby hugged herself, listening intently to his words.

"Well, eventually, Ms. Matthews called me in. I was failing at school, bit by bit. I swore I wasn't going to tell anyone what I was feeling. Because I'm not sure I knew what I was feeling, exactly."

Ruby felt a weight lift off her chest. She knew what he meant. She had no idea he had felt that way, too. "But you did tell her?"

He nodded. "Yeah. For like an hour I was there, just talking and talking. It felt better after," he tapped his head and then his heart, "but not like everything was okay. Just... better."

"I guess what I'm having are nightmares, too. Just different ones."

Alex didn't judge her or assess her words. He just sat there, letting her process her thoughts. She needed that.

"It's okay, Ruby. Everything you feel. It's okay."

But she didn't want to admit just yet all of her feelings. Instead, she nodded, still trying to be strong.

Ruby hadn't realized how much she needed someone who already knew what loss felt like. Not just the quiet kind you carry, but the kind that clings to you when you're alone in your room and every sound feels like it might break you. Alex, in his calm, no-pressure way, didn't just listen—he understood. And somehow, that made everything she was feeling feel a little less heavy.

She thought it odd, too, that for so long she had been strong. Until last night. Now, she felt anything but in control.

Ruby studied her friend's face, seeing no judgment there, only genuine concern. She thought about how Alex had changed over the past year, how he'd seemed to find his footing again after his loss. "Did you tell him about everything? Even the stuff that made no sense?"

"Everything," Alex confirmed. "That's kind of the point. They help you make sense of it."

The first bell rang, startling them both. As they walked to class, Ruby found herself considering the possibility. Maybe it was time to stop running from her feelings. Maybe it was time to face them head-on.

Chapter 6

Cracks in the Real World

T he day dragged on at school; Ruby couldn't concentrate. Her mind kept drifting back to the dream city. During lunch she heard snippets of conversation that seemed oddly familiar—as if pieces of her dream world were leaking into reality. *Inferno's my name... Oh, forgive me Lady Sapphire...*

Sapphire lives in that tower over there...!

Sitting on the bleachers during lunch, her tray of untouched food beside her, Ruby was pretending to watch Aqua, who was scrolling through her phone. But her mind was distracted and not focussed on her friend. Nevertheless, she did hear Aqua's laughter, which occasionally broke the silence between them. Aqua began to share memes and videos with Ruby.

"Ruby, check this out," Aqua said, holding up her phone. "This guy literally fell off his skateboard right into a fountain."

Ruby smiled faintly but didn't look very closely. She thought about telling Aqua about her dream. After all,

Aqua was her best friend. But the words caught in her throat.

"What's up with you today?" Aqua asked, her brow furrowing as she set her phone down. "You've been spaced out all week."

Ruby hesitated, her fingers gripping the edge of the bleacher. "It's... nothing. Just school stuff, I guess."

Aqua tilted her head, unconvinced. "Come on, Rubes. I know when something's bugging you. Spill."

Ruby looked down at her hands. Aqua was her best friend, but the idea of sharing something so personal, so weird, felt like stepping off a cliff. What if Aqua thought she was crazy? What if she laughed? Ruby's fear of Aqua rejecting her concern over a dream was somehow overwhelming, and Ruby figured it best to not disclose the truth for now.

Alina V. Shi

"It's really nothing," Ruby said finally, forcing a smile. "Just stressed, you know?"

Aqua nodded, seemingly satisfied. But as she returned to her phone, Ruby felt a pang of guilt. Aqua was her best friend, but somehow, Ruby couldn't bring herself to open up to her.

"Hey Ruby," interrupted Sarah from science class. "You coming to the party tonight?"

Ruby blinked, confused. "What party?"

"Jake's birthday party! The one everyone's talking about?" Sarah adjusted the phone and water bottle in her hands.

"C'mon, Rubes, you gotta go!" Aqua stated, overhearing Sarah. "I'll be there."

Ruby hadn't heard about it, but she nodded anyway. "Yeah, sure. Sounds fun."

Sarah smiled and walked away. *Maybe a party would be a good distraction for me. Maybe it will help me figure things out.*

After school, the gym echoed with the sharp squeak of sneakers and the rhythmic drumming of basketballs hitting the hardwood floor. Ruby stood at the free-throw line, her palms slick with sweat as her teammates called out words of encouragement.

"Come on, Ruby! Just focus!" her coach shouted from the sidelines.

Ruby tried to drown out the noise, but her mind was racing. The dream of Sapphire City lingered in her thoughts, its vividness unsettling. Every time she closed her eyes, instead of her usual calm and confident demeanor for her sporting events, she saw Sapphire's face, her superior smile, and the city that felt so tied to her own chaotic emotions.

She dribbled the ball, trying to concentrate, but a voice in her head whispered, *You're going to miss. You always mess things up when it counts.*

Just as she came around and was poised to take the shot, her grip faltered, and when she released the ball, it spun awkwardly, hitting the rim before bouncing off. A groan erupted from her teammates.

"Shake it off, Ruby!" Alex, who was seated on the bench, called out. His voice was warm and supportive, but she could feel the disappointment radiating from the rest of the team.

Practice continued, but Ruby's performance didn't improve. Her passes were sloppy, her defense was slow, and every missed shot gnawed at her confidence. She grew worried that her teammates were increasingly frustrated with her, but the more she tried to correct her poor play, the worse it got.

At one point, one of the captains on her team stopped passing the ball to her altogether, and Ruby knew it was just a matter of time. If this level of poor performance continued, she would be benched.

At the end of the session, her coach pulled her aside.

"Ruby, what's going on with you? You're one of our best players, but today... it's like your head wasn't in the game," he said, his tone gentle but firm.

"I'm sorry, Coach," Ruby muttered, avoiding his gaze. "I just... I guess I have a lot on my mind."

"Well, whatever it is, you need to

sort it out. The team's counting on you. We've got a big game on Friday."

Ruby nodded, feeling the weight of his words pressing down on her. She left the gym that evening with her shoulders slumped, wondering if she would ever feel like herself again.

At home, Ruby was in her room when she heard the front door slam and the sound of sobbing echoing through the house. She rushed out to find Mia sitting on the hallway floor, her backpack discarded, her face buried in her hands.

"Mia, what's wrong?" Ruby knelt beside her, her heart sinking.

"They—" Mia choked on a sob. "They said I'm weird. Just because..." A sob caught in her throat, and she had to pause. She continued with a broken sentence, words intertwined with bouts of uncontrollable sobbing.

"Just... because... I'm the girl... with the... broken family!"

Ruby's chest tightened in anger: *how dare they make fun of my sister for this?* She knew that seeing her older sister angry right now would not help, so she focused on her breath and pushed her anger aside.

Gently pulling Mia into a hug, Ruby tenderly said, "Kids can be cruel, Mia. I am so sorry about what you went through today, but that doesn't mean what they say is true."

Mia clung to her like a boat moored to a dock during a storm, her sobs eventually quieting. "I just want us to be normal, like other families."

Ruby swallowed hard, fighting her own emotions. "Well... we might not be like some other families, but you know what? That doesn't mean we're not strong." Ruby peered deeply into Mia's eyes for a moment before continuing. "You're strong, Mia. *We are both strong.* Always remember that. We're stronger than you know."

Mia sniffled and then pulled back to look at Ruby. "I don't want to be strong. I just want my friends to be nice to me."

"You know, you can't control how they act towards you, Mia. If they can't be nice, maybe they aren't really your friends." Ruby gently pushed Mia's hair out of her eyes. "But you know what? You'll find others who will be nice to you, and those may turn out to be your *true* friends. And until then, you need to remember that you are strong enough to handle things when these other kids are acting so foolishly."

Peering deeply into her older sister's eyes, Mia asked, "Do you really think I'm that strong?"

Ruby smiled. "I know you are. And I promise, no matter what, we're going to be okay." Ruby embraced Mia with a firm hug, and for the first time in a long time, Mia smiled and wrapped her arms around Ruby's back.

Ruby suddenly realized how important it was for Mia to have an older sister who had both patience and understanding. She wanted Mia to know that she was going to try harder to be the older sister that Mia needed right now.

"Mia," she began, "I also just want you to know that I am sorry, and that I know how hard things have been around here lately. I haven't always been the kind of sister you need, and I just... I guess I want to say that I don't always know how to show you how much I care about you. But I'm going to try to always be a better sister for you."

Mia looked up, surprised. "It's okay, Ruby... I'm sorry too."

Seeing Mia smiling at her warmed Ruby's heart.

Ruby thought she heard something and glanced towards the hallway to see their mother standing behind them, her face tight with a mix of both pride and guilt. Ruby smiled at her mom and understood that she was stepping into a role her mother should have filled long before. It did not matter at this moment, and for the first time since she lost her dad and brother, Ruby felt the stirrings of resolve.

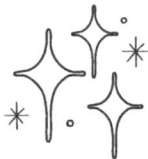

Chapter 7

Sapphire

An hour later, Ruby was standing outside of Jake's house feeling nervous, though she didn't quite know why. The bass of electronic dance music thumped from inside and lights flashed through the windows. Finally, she sucked in a deep breath and pushed the door open.

Inside, the party was in full swing. People were dancing, talking, having a great time. She saw Alex near the snack table, leaning casually against the wall, and made her way over to him.

"Hey! You made it," he said with a smile.

"Yeah," Ruby replied, looking around. "It's packed."

Alex nodded. "For sure, Jake really knows how to throw bangers."

They mixed their drinks—soda and juices—and made small talk for a while. Ruby started to relax more than she thought she would—like the things of her dreams were just that: dreams and nothing more.

But it didn't last. Ruby was talking with friends when Aqua entered the house. Ruby's temples suddenly throbbed like someone was driving nails into her skull—*not again.* Was she seeing things? The music warped, bass notes slowing to funeral-drum tempo. Lights flickered, and for a heartbeat, the party smelled like the ocean cliff where Dad used to take them. Salt. Pine. Gone.

Then she saw her—perched on Jake's couch like a crow on a power line. Sapphire lounged, sipping something that bubbled black. No one else noticed her fingers were too long, or how the drink ate through the glass she clutched.

Ruby's heartbeat quickened as she wiped at her eyes, and then, just as suddenly as she had appeared, Sapphire was gone. In a panic, she looked around to find Alex standing several feet away near the hallway. Approaching him, Ruby grabbed his arm.

"Did you see that?" she asked, her voice trembling.

He frowned at her. "See what?"

"Sapphire," Ruby replied shakily through tight lips. "She—she was just there."

Alex paused for a moment before he spoke again slowly. "Ruby... maybe you should sit down..."

She nodded dumbly in agreement as he led her over to a quiet corner where they both sat on a couch. Trying hard to even out her anxious and somewhat spastic breathing patterns, she couldn't make sense of any of this.

What was going on?

"I see things, Alex," Ruby confessed. "I don't know what's real."

Alex squeezed her hand. "We'll figure this out, Ruby. You're not alone. I am right here with you."

Ruby nodded, thankful for his support. Ruby had wanted to tell Aqua about her dream but had feared her best friend would not understand her vulnerability or take her seriously. With Alex, she realized there was no fear of rejection. Her comfort with Alex came from a place of shared experiences, something they'd had ever since lower school. With Alex, she had always discussed her dreams and her doubts, as he had done with her.

As they sat close together on the couch, Ruby felt reassured by Alex's presence and his support. With her best girlfriends, there was a sort of unspoken competitive spirit between them. Something about each of them left her feeling they had a need to keep up with one another, to maintain the status quo of confidence and maturity. So, in that moment when she saw Sapphire, Ruby was grateful that Alex was right there for her, and she realized just how much she valued their friendship.

"Maybe we should get you home," Alex finally suggested, and she agreed.

They arrived at her house, and Ruby paused outside the front door. "Thanks for walking me home," she said quietly. She paused and looked at his bright eyes. "In fact, thanks for all you do. I guess I don't tell you this so often, but I'm glad for your support and friendship."

"No problem," Alex said. He paused as if thinking about what he wanted to say. "I think you're awesome too, Ruby." He studied her face and then offered a smile. "Get some rest, okay? I'll check on you tomorrow."

Ruby gave him a small smile and went inside.

The house was dark and still. She tiptoed up to her room, careful not to wake her mother or Mia. Shadow greeted her with a soft purr, twining around her legs. Ruby picked him up and held him close, finding solace in the warm embrace. *I may as well try to study a little for tomorrow's exam, so I don't have to stress about it so much in the morning.*

She went to her desk and opened her backpack. Taking out her history textbook, Ruby opened it to Chapter Six. But even though she read the opening paragraph of her textbook several times, she may as well have been trying to read with her eyes shut—*nothing reached her brain!*

All she wanted to think about was the dream world she'd slipped into the night before. Who were those people in the dream? And what did it all mean?

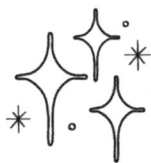

Chapter 8

Facing Inferno

S taring at the open textbook in front of her, the words seemed to just blur together on the page. Her history test was tomorrow, but no matter how hard she tried to focus, her mind kept drifting. She tapped her pencil against the desk, her frustration building.

"You'll fail," a familiar and menacing voice whispered.

No, no, no! This wasn't happening—was she dreaming again?

Ruby's head snapped up, her breath catching in her throat. Across the room, a figure stood in the shadows, their outline glowing faintly in a fiery red. Ruby knew it was Inferno, her best friend's counterpart from her dreamworld. The contentious smirk on her face was sharp and unrelenting.

"Why are you here?" Ruby's voice was low and trembling. "Just leave me alone and go back to your own world."

"What about *your* world?" Inferno asked, pointing a blazing, accusatory finger at Ruby. "Who's gonna make your world all better for you?"

"Get out—I mean it!" Ruby whispered fiercely.

"Make me!" Inferno countered smugly.

For a moment, Ruby considered throwing her textbook at Inferno to see if it would hit her or go right through her, but she did not want to risk waking Mia or her mom. Instead, she shook her head to try to clear her thoughts. "This isn't real."

"Oh, I'm very real," Inferno gloated, stepping closer. "I'm the part of you that's tired of pretending everything's fine. Why study? Why bother? You're just going to mess up anyway."

Ruby clenched her fists, her nails digging into her palms. "You don't know that."

Inferno laughed, the sound echoing in Ruby's mind. "I know you, Ruby. I *am* you. And you can't get rid of me until you face what's really eating you up inside."

Before Ruby could respond, Inferno vanished just as quickly as she had appeared. The room felt eerily quiet. Ruby's heart raced.

"This didn't happen," she muttered. "I'm just tired."

She turned back to her textbook, but the words danced on the page before her eyes. Her mind was spinning. As she felt her frustration boiling over, she slammed her book shut.

She stood and found herself drifting over to the corner of the room Inferno had just occupied. She ruffled the curtain and kicked at the carpeting, then touched one of the walls. But there was nothing, no sign of the petulant, bothersome figure.

Exhausted, Ruby collapsed onto her bed. Soon, Shadow came out from beneath the bed and joined her, curling up beside her. As always, Ruby was grateful for his presence and reached out to rub behind his ears. Even after a few minutes, however, she couldn't shake the feeling that something was still dreadfully wrong. Ruby squeezed her eyes shut until colors burst behind her lids.

One... two...

Shadow's purr melted into the city's mechanical hum.

Three...

Her mattress became concrete. Cold seeped through her clothes.

She opened her eyes to fractured neon. The city always knew when she was lying.

Once again, she stood in those same futuristic streets, now hauntingly empty. She wandered through them, feeling adrift and uneasy. Just when she was feeling burdened by the fact that nobody was around, she heard footsteps behind her. When she whirled around, Sapphire was standing before her, looking cool as ever.

Ruby'd had enough of this. *"Why are you doing this?"* she demanded. Her voice was pinched, unsteady as fear and fury washed through her.

Sapphire smirked slightly. "You just don't get it, do you?" She took two authoritative loops around Ruby. "This isn't about you, girl... *it's about all of us."*

Growing more confused by the second, Ruby asked, "What do you mean?"

"Let me spell it out for you." Stepping right up to Ruby, Sapphire replied, "Your emotions shape this world: your fear... your anger... your sadness. They all feed into a crescendo of things that you try holding back, and this is what is causing all this chaos!!!"

Ruby was about to protest, but Sapphire stopped her by declaring, "The only way to stop all of this is by accepting and then confronting your feelings head-on!!!"

Ruby stared at Sapphire and finally allowed what she was saying to sink in. "*But how?* How am I supposed to do that?"

Sapphire's expression softened a little. "Begin with accepting that you have these feelings inside of you. You have to stop hiding away from hard emotions and learn to embrace them instead. That is when you, *and only you*, can take charge of all the obstacles in your life. The obstacles cause them to exist."

The ground began shaking again. Large crevices split the streets wide open once again. Ruby's heart raced as the endless void was ripping right towards her, threatening to engulf her in seconds. If Sapphire was right, Ruby herself controlled the void and the entire city, and the only way to stop all the insanity was by doing what Sapphire had suggested. She drew a deep breath and tried to steady her nerves.

"Fine!" Ruby said, and she then felt a surge of determination welling up within her that was stronger than anything she had ever felt before. "I will try."

Sapphire nodded approvingly and then winked at her. At that very moment, everything shattered around them in a cascade of broken glass and twisted metal.

Ruby woke up with a jolt.

She sat upright and realized she was back in her own bed. Holding her chest, she thought about her father and brother once again, and the great misfortune her family had suffered.

She considered her mother's drinking, along with the emptiness her mother tried to hide day in and day out. As she faced all of it, tears streamed down Ruby's cheeks.

Shadow mewed softly, sensing Ruby's pain. The girl reached out for him and stroked his silky fur, finding solace once again in the cat's presence. She considered that her dream *was real* after all. Sapphire's words still rang in her ears.

Getting up, she glanced through the window where dawn was breaking on the horizon and a strange lucidity overcame her. She took in a deep breath. Then, she knew what she had to do.

After she finished getting dressed, she went downstairs. Her mom was still asleep as Mia ate breakfast quietly.

"Morning," Ruby said, her voice

gentle, as she slipped into the chair next to her sister.

Mia glanced up; her face still puffy from sleep but more relaxed than Ruby had seen in a while. "Morning," she replied, her tone lighter than usual.

Ruby reached for the cereal box and poured herself a bowl, the familiar clinking of the spoon filling the silence. She hesitated for a moment, then nudged Mia's plate. "You forgot the butter on your toast. It's a rookie mistake."

Mia rolled her eyes but smiled. "Maybe I like it this way."

Ruby smirked. "Or maybe you're just lazy."

Mia laughed softly, and Ruby felt a flicker of relief. After everything, this felt... normal. Like a small piece of the sisterhood they had been missing was finally sliding back into place.

Ruby leaned her elbows on the table. "Hey, remember last summer? When we tried to bake cookies, and you kept sneaking the chocolate chips?"

Mia grinned. "You mean when you burnt the cookies because you forgot the timer?"

"Minor detail," Ruby said, waving her hand. "The point is, I saved the day with my epic frosting skills."

Mia laughed again, shaking her head. "Your frosting was just melted chocolate. That doesn't count as *skills*."

"Hey, it was innovative!" Ruby shot back, her mock indignation earning a playful shove from Mia.

In the hallway, Ruby noticed their mother leaning against the doorway, mostly in shadows. It looked like she'd been woken up by the sound of their voices and had come downstairs to find them laughing. She stayed still, watching her daughters with an expression of guilt and longing.

Shadow padded into the kitchen, hopping onto Mia's lap. She stroked him absentmindedly, her smile lingering.

"You know," Ruby said, breaking the quiet, "we should try baking those cookies again sometime. No burnt ones this time. I promise."

"Only if I get to eat the chocolate chips," Mia said, her eyes sparkling.

"Deal," Ruby said, grinning.

Their mother took a step back, retreating to her room, but not before one last glance at her daughters. For the first time in a long time, the house felt alive—not with tension, but with something lighter, something hopeful.

Chapter 9

Moving Through Doubt

A week later, Ruby sat in the library, her laptop glowing softly in the dim light. The deadline for her English paper was looming, but her progress was agonizingly slow. The assignment was to write a short discourse about how one might overcome obstacles. Her cursor blinked mockingly at the top of a blank document.

"Come on, Ruby," she muttered to herself. "Just write something."

She typed a sentence, then deleted it. Typed another, then erased that too. Every word felt wrong, like it wasn't good enough.

"You're wasting your time," a familiar voice said.

Ruby froze. When she looked up, Sapphire was sitting across from her, her chin resting on her hand. Her blue hair shimmered under the library lights.

"You're back," Ruby said, her voice filled with a mix of irritation and exhaustion. "Great."

"I never left," Sapphire replied with a sly smile. "You can't escape me, Ruby.

You're trying so hard to ignore your feelings, but it's not going to work. You'll keep spinning your wheels until you deal with the truth."

"What truth?" Ruby snapped. "That everything still sucks even though Mom and Mia are nicer to me? That I'm angry all the time about Dad and Liam? What good does it do to dwell on that?"

"That's where you are all wrong ... it's not about dwelling," Sapphire said, her tone softening. "It's about accepting. Your feelings don't go away just because you ignore them. The only way to move through them is to embrace them."

Ruby stared at Sapphire, her anger simmering beneath the surface. But as the words sank in, she felt a flicker of understanding. She didn't have to let her emotions control her, but she couldn't keep running from them either. One good deed didn't mean that all the damage in her house was healed.

When Ruby blinked, Sapphire was gone. The library was quiet again, save for the faint hum of computers. Ruby exhaled unevenly and then turned back to her laptop. Slowly, tentatively, she began to write.

As she looked at the words on the page a moment later, she realized that she was writing about how a person might need to ask for help when they find there is an obstacle in their life that is very difficult for them to overcome.

She didn't want to embrace her feelings because when she had in the past, they had led her to a roadblock—an uncertainty about what to do with the one obstacle she could not yet fathom how to work through. As Ruby reread her own words, she realized that she was done with holding onto her own pride and that she needed to seek help herself.

Ruby's mind drifted back to a quiet evening not long after the funeral. The house was dark except for the faint glow from the kitchen. She had lingered in the doorway, watching her mother sit at the table, a glass of wine in hand, staring at a framed photo of Dad and Liam.

Ruby hesitated, gripping the edge of the doorframe. Her chest felt tight, the words she wanted to say caught in her throat. Finally, she stepped forward. "Mom?"

Her mother didn't look up. "What is it, Ruby?" Her voice was distant, thin, like a frayed thread barely visible.

Ruby edged closer, her fingers twisting the hem of her sweater. "I... I miss them," she said softly.

Her mother's hand tightened around the glass. The faint clink of her nails against the stem echoed in the silence. "Me too," she murmured, her gaze fixed on the photo.

Ruby shuffled her feet, searching for the right words. "It just feels like... like they should still be here, you know?" Her voice wavered. "Sometimes it hurts so much, I don't know what to do."

Her mother finally looked at her, her eyes rimmed with red. For a moment, Ruby thought she might reach out, say something, anything. But her mother's expression crumpled, and she turned away, covering her face with one hand.

"I can't," her mother whispered. Her shoulders shook as she drew in a ragged breath. "I can't do this right now, Ruby."

Ruby froze, the small flicker of hope extinguished. She stood there, watching her mother dissolve into quiet sobs, the glass trembling in her hand.

Ruby's own hands balled into fists at her sides. She wanted to cry, to scream, to make her mother see how much she needed her. But instead, she nodded, her throat burning. "Okay," she said, her voice barely audible.

She turned and walked away, her footsteps silent on the floor. In her room, she sat on the edge of her bed, staring at her hands. She hadn't cried. She couldn't. Her mother's sorrow was a wall Ruby couldn't climb, and that night, she decided not to try again.

Back in the library, Ruby wiped her eyes with the back of her hand. She looked at the screen and reread the part she had typed about needing to ask for help sometimes.

Committing to a course of action, she left the library and scheduled a visit with the guidance counselor for the following Monday....

The following week, Ruby sat stiffly in the chair across from Ms. Carter, the school counselor, her hands clasped tightly in her lap. The room was small but welcoming, with soft lighting and a wall of bookshelves filled with titles about self-help and personal growth. A potted plant sat by the window, its leaves curling toward the sunlight. Shadow's absence felt sharp, like a missing piece of armor.

"So, Ruby," Ms. Carter began, her voice calm and even, "how are you feeling today?"

Ruby hesitated, her fingers clenching around each other into a tight ball. She thought about the dream, about Sapphire and Inferno, about the mess of emotions she didn't know how to handle. But how could she explain any of that without sounding crazy?

"I... I've just been feeling off," she finally said, her voice barely above a whisper.

"Off how?" Ms. Carter asked gently.

Ruby fidgeted, searching for the right words. "Like... everything is too much. Like I'm supposed to keep it all together, but I'm not doing a very good job."

Ms. Carter nodded again. "That's a hard place to be. It sounds like you're carrying a lot right now."

Ruby's chest tightened. How could she finally admit to the thing which troubled her most? She had kept it hidden inside for so long because she did not want to bother anyone with how difficult this burden had been for her to bear.

With nowhere else to turn, Ruby knew she had no choice. "I miss my dad and Liam," she blurted out, the words tumbling out before she could stop them. Her voice cracked, and she looked away, embarrassed.

"It's okay to miss them," Ms. Carter said softly. "It's okay to feel sad or even angry about what happened. Those feelings are normal."

Ruby bit her lip, her vision blurring with unshed tears. "I just... I feel like I have to be strong for everyone. For my mom, for Mia. But I'm not strong. I'm just... tired."

Ms. Carter leaned forward slightly, her expression kind. "Ruby, being strong doesn't mean ignoring how you feel. It means acknowledging those feelings and finding a way to face them. And you don't have to do it alone."

The tears spilled over then, and Ruby quickly wiped them away, her face burning with shame. But Ms. Carter didn't seem to judge her. She handed Ruby a tissue and waited patiently.

For the first time in a long time, Ruby let herself cry. It wasn't a loud or dramatic cry, but a quiet, cathartic release. When the tears finally stopped, she felt lighter, as though a weight had been lifted.

"Thank you," Ruby said quietly, her voice hoarse.

"You're welcome," Ms. Carter replied with a small smile. "This is just the beginning, Ruby. It's going to take time, but you're already taking the first step by being here."

Ruby nodded, a small spark of hope flickering in her chest. Maybe Ms. Carter was right. Maybe she didn't have to carry everything alone.

As she left the counselor's office, the world outside seemed a little less heavy, and for the first time in a while, *Ruby felt like she could breathe.*

The clatter of plastic trays and burst of laughter from the next table made Ruby wince. She poked at her sandwich with one finger, watching the wheat bread compress and spring back like a sponge. The cafeteria smelled of overcooked fries and floor cleaner, making her stomach turn.

"—and then Sarah said her parents are going away for the weekend, so the whole house will be—" Aqua's voice cut through the noise, then stopped abruptly. A french fry bounced off Ruby's forehead.

Ruby blinked, looking up to find Aqua staring at her with narrowed eyes. "Did you just throw a fry at me?"

"Desperate times." Aqua leaned forward, her dark hair falling across one eye. She brushed it back with an impatient gesture. "That's the third time you've zoned out in ten minutes. What's going on in that head of yours?"

Ruby's fingers found the wrapper of her sandwich, methodically tearing it into tiny strips. "Just tired."

"Right." Aqua's tone was flat. She reached across the table and stilled Ruby's hands. Her fingers were warm against Ruby's cold ones. "Because 'tired' totally explains why you've been dodging my texts, canceling our movie nights, and basically turning into a ghost for the past three weeks."

Ruby pulled her hands away, letting the paper pieces scatter across her tray. The sandwich sat untouched, a testament to conversations not happening. "I'm not—"

"If you say 'I'm fine' one more time, I swear I'll dump this entire carton of milk over your head." Aqua's voice wavered between humor and hurt. She pushed her tray aside and folded her arms on the table, leaning closer. "Remember in seventh grade, when Jenny Thompson told everyone I still slept with a nightlight?"

The memory flickered: Aqua crying in the girls' bathroom, Ruby standing guard at the door, plotting revenge involving Jenny's gym clothes and a bottle of pickle juice. "Of course."

"And remember what you told me?"

Ruby's throat tightened. "That she was stupid, and real friends don't judge each other."

"Exactly." Aqua's eyes softened. "So why are you judging me now?"

"I'm not—"

"You are. You're judging me, thinking I can't handle whatever's going on with you." Aqua's hand shot out again, this time gripping Ruby's wrist. "Did I do something wrong? Are you mad at me?"

"No!" The word came out too loud. A few heads turned their way, and Ruby lowered her voice. "No, Aqua. You didn't do anything."

"Then what?" Aqua's grip loosened but didn't let go. "Because I feel like I'm watching my best friend disappear, and I don't know how to stop it."

The fluorescent lights buzzed overhead, harsh and unforgiving. Ruby stared at Aqua's hand on her wrist, at the familiar silver bracelet she'd given her for her fourteenth birthday. Her vision blurred.

"I'm seeing Ms. Carter," she whispered, the words feeling like glass in her throat.

Aqua's hand tightened briefly, then relaxed. "The counselor?"

Ruby nodded, still not looking up. Her heart pounded against her ribs like it was trying to escape.

"Okay," Aqua said softly. Then again, firmer: "Okay. That's... that's good, Ruby. But why couldn't you tell me?"

"Because..." Ruby's voice cracked. She pulled her hand away and pressed her palms against her eyes. "Because I'm supposed to be the strong one. I'm supposed to have it together. I'm not supposed to be—"

"Human?" Aqua's chair scraped against the floor. A moment later, Ruby felt arms wrap around her shoulders. Aqua's familiar coconut shampoo filled her nose as her friend hugged her tight. "News flash, genius. You're allowed to fall apart sometimes. And I'm allowed to help put you back together."

Ruby let out a shaky breath, her hands dropping to her lap. Around them, the cafeteria continued its chaotic dance of social interactions and half-eaten lunches, but in their little bubble, something shifted. Like a window being opened after a long winter, letting in fresh air.

"I see things sometimes," Ruby whispered into Aqua's shoulder. "When I dream. And sometimes... sometimes when I'm awake too."

Aqua pulled back just enough to look at her face, no judgment in her expression. Just concern, and something that looked a lot like love. "Tell me?"

Ruby glanced around the crowded cafeteria, at the sea of faces absorbed in their own dramas and dreams. "Not here. But... maybe after school?"

Aqua smiled, relief brightening her

entire face. "My place? Mom's making her famous mac and cheese."

"With the crispy breadcrumb thing on top?"

"Obviously. What are we, savages?"

Ruby laughed, the sound surprising her with its authenticity. The weight in her chest felt a little lighter. The sandwich on her tray still sat untouched, but now she reached for it, suddenly hungry.

"Ruby?" Aqua said as she returned to her seat.

"Yeah?"

"Whatever you're seeing, whatever you're going through? We'll figure it out together. Okay?"

Ruby took a bite of her sandwich. "Okay."

Above them, the fluorescent lights still buzzed, but somehow, they seemed a little less harsh, a little more like stars.

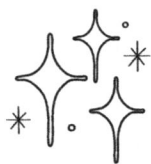

Chapter 10

Facing Feelings

After her second session with Ms. Carter, Ruby started journaling—not because she wanted to, but because it felt safer than speaking out loud.

The pages didn't judge. They just held things.

Entry 1

Ms. Carter gave me this notebook. Said I didn't have to write in it, but sometimes thoughts settle better on paper. I didn't think I'd use it. But here I am.

Today she asked me what I was afraid of. I said spiders. She didn't laugh, which was cool. But she looked at me like she knew that wasn't the real answer.

The truth is, I think I'm afraid that if I feel all the things I've been trying not to feel, I'll come apart.

Entry 3

Cried in session today. Couldn't stop once I started. I felt embarrassed. But Ms. Carter just handed me a tissue and waited. It felt weirdly okay, being seen like that. Not dramatic. Just... honest.

I told her about the dreams. Not all of them, just the ones with the fire. She nodded like it made perfect sense. Like she had walked through fire too.

Entry 7

We talked about forgiveness. Not the cheesy kind. The kind that doesn't excuse anything but lets you breathe again.

I told her I don't know if I can forgive my mom. Ms. Carter said I don't have to decide that now. Just that it's okay to hold space for the question.

Holding space is harder than it sounds.

Entry 10

I haven't dreamed of Inferno in a while. Or maybe I have and just didn't wake up afraid.

It's not that everything's better. But when I breathe in, I don't feel like I'm stealing air. I think that counts as progress.

Entry 12 — Thursday Night

I saw someone at school today who looked like Dad. Just for a second. He was getting coffee in the teacher's lounge window, and the way he stood—the slouch in his back—it made my stomach drop.

I think that's the worst part. He's not here, but parts of him are everywhere.

Entry 13 — Lunchtime

I sat alone today. Not because no one asked—Alex waved me over—but I just didn't want to talk. It's weird. I'm tired of being lonely, but sometimes the idea of being around people feels heavier than the loneliness itself.

Ms. Carter would probably say that's a sign I need rest, not isolation. I can almost hear her voice in my head.

That's either progress or a side effect of too much journaling.

Entry 15 — After walking Mia to bed

Mia held my hand for a second longer than usual tonight. I didn't say anything. Just squeezed back.

I wish I'd had someone to do that for me when I was her age. Maybe I did and just didn't notice. Or maybe that's why I'm here now.

◈ ✳ ◈ ✳ ◈

Ruby sat alone under the bleachers after gym class, her forehead pressed against her knees. She had just bombed another quiz and the weight of everything was pressing on her like a lead blanket.

"Okay, no more avoiding it." Aqua's voice cut through the quiet. Ruby looked up, startled. Aqua stood there, arms crossed, her usual playful demeanor gone. "I've been trying to give you space after you told me about your dream and seeing the counselor, but I can't keep pretending everything's fine. You're... different."

Ruby swallowed hard. "Aqua, I'm just tired."

"No, Ruby. You've been shutting me out for weeks. I miss my best friend."

Ruby looked away, guilt washing over her. "I didn't mean to push you away. I just... I didn't know how to explain exactly what's been happening."

Aqua knelt beside her. "Well, try harder. Because I've been sitting in silence thinking I did something wrong. And if you're hurting, I want to be there. That's what friends do."

Ruby hesitated, then let out a long breath. "It's been a mess in my head. Dreams... memories. More than what I told you already. I feel like I'm losing it. And I didn't think anyone would understand."

Aqua softened, resting a hand on Ruby's arm. "You should've told me more. I might not have all the answers, but I'm not afraid of your mess. I'm your friend, Rubes. You don't have to go through this alone."

A small tear rolled down Ruby's cheek. She nodded. "Okay. I'll try."

Aqua smiled. "Good. Now come on. My mom made those ridiculous marshmallow squares again. Let's go eat sugar and figure this out together."

Ruby straightened her back and stood up from the grass. She brushed dirt from her knees, squared her shoulders, and met Aqua's eyes with a small but steady nod. Something inside her had shifted—like a crack of sunlight slipping through after a long storm.

Ruby worked on embracing feelings throughout the next several weeks: talking with Ms. Carter about grief and anger management; spending as much time around Mia as possible, trying to rebuild whatever they once had together; and even letting her mom know that it was difficult to feel any patience or respect for her when she was drinking.

That night, she dreamed again.

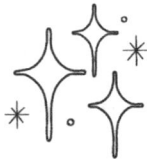

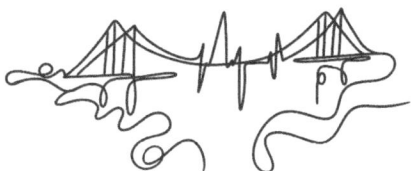

Chapter 11

Bridges and Mirrors

The air shimmered when Ruby stepped into Sapphire City again.

It was different this time—quieter, the streets dimmed like stage lights waiting for the cue. Instead of glass towers stretching toward the sky, Ruby stood at the edge of a wide, silvery river. No current. No sound. Just stillness.

Ahead, a bridge arched over the water. But it wasn't stone or steel—it was made of mirrors.

Every panel reflected a different version of her: Ruby laughing as a child, Ruby crying into her pillow, Ruby running down a hallway, Ruby standing perfectly still. The bridge pulsed faintly beneath her feet, like it had a heartbeat of its own.

Sapphire appeared beside her, hands clasped behind her back.

"You're almost through, you know," she said quietly. "But you can't leave this place until you cross the bridge."

"What happens if I fall?"

"Then you'll meet the version of yourself you've been trying hardest to avoid."

Ruby didn't respond. She stepped forward.

Each mirror buzzed as she passed, reflecting not just memories, but interpretations—the way she saw herself in those moments. Weak. Angry. Alone. The reflections whispered things she'd heard in her own mind too many times.

You're not enough.

You let them down.

You're the reason she drinks.

Her steps faltered. The glass beneath her feet creaked.

Then—another voice. Not Sapphire's. Not Inferno's. Her own.

You're still here.

The bridge steadied.

You're walking.

And she was.

You don't have to believe every version of yourself you've ever been.

When she reached the other side, she was crying—but not afraid.

Sapphire stood waiting. She gave a small nod.

"You're almost done."

Chapter 12

First Steps Forward

W eeks passed. Not all days were good, but some were. And that was new.

Ruby didn't want to speak first. She sat in a blue plastic chair, part of a lopsided circle in the school's resource center, surrounded by five other students. A poster on the wall read: *"Healing isn't linear."* She kept her eyes on it like it might hand her the right words if she stared long enough.

Ms. Carter introduced everyone, but Ruby barely caught the others' names. What she did catch were the twitches—knees bouncing, fingers tapping, arms crossed over chests. Everyone here was hiding in plain sight.

When it came time to share, a boy with a buzzcut muttered something about being tired. A girl with chipped purple nail polish talked about how quiet her house had become since her brother left for rehab.

Then it was Ruby's turn. She thought about saying "I'm fine." She thought about lying. But instead, her own voice surprised her.

"I used to dream about a city falling apart. Like, literally cracking open. And someone told me it was my fault because I wouldn't feel what I needed to feel."

A silence settled over the group. Not cold. Not confused. Just... listening.

"I guess I'm here to try and stop the ground from falling out beneath me."

No one laughed. No one shifted away. Ms. Carter gave a small nod, like Ruby had spoken in a language she understood fluently.

Ruby exhaled. Maybe this circle of strangers wasn't so strange after all.

That night, dinner was just toast and scrambled eggs.

But they were all sitting at the table—Ruby, Mia, and their mother.

No one had wine. No one was shouting. No one flinched when someone dropped a fork.

Mia was talking about her art project. Ruby was listening. Their mom was... trying. Not perfect. But trying.

When Ruby offered to do the dishes and her mom said, "We'll do them together," something in Ruby's chest clicked into place. Not healed. But mending.

Chapter 13

Victory on the Court

I t was another Friday night, and the gym was alive with energy. The rivalry game this week had drawn a crowd, and the bleachers were packed with cheering students and parents. Ruby stood in the huddle with her teammates, her heart pounding as the coach outlined their strategy for the final quarter.

They were down by six points, and Ruby could feel the pressure. But something was different this time. She had spent the past few days thinking about Sapphire's words: *Accept your feelings. Don't run from them.*

Standing on the court now, she took a deep breath and let herself feel everything—the fear of failure, the lingering sadness over the loss of her father and brother, the frustration of her mom's drinking. Instead of pushing it all away, she embraced her true feelings. And as she did, she felt a strange sense of calm settle over her.

The whistle blew, and the game resumed. Ruby moved with newfound confidence, her steps light and purposeful. She made a clean pass to a teammate, then darted to an open spot on the court. When the ball came back to her, she didn't hesitate, and her skills came through naturally. Her shot arced perfectly through the air, swishing through the net.

"Yes!" she heard Alex yell from the stands.

The momentum started to shift slowly in their favor, and yet the rival team began to rise to the occasion, as well. As the fourth quarter wound down, Ruby's defense was sharp, her passes precise, and her shots on target. With ten seconds left on the clock, their team was down by one point. The ball was in Ruby's hands. She drove towards the opponent's basket, weaving through and past defenders.

A quick glance at the clock showed three seconds remaining, and there would be no time for anything else. As she drew up towards the net, she knew their only hope was for her to make a layup. Her feet took to the air as she raised the ball up and around with her right arm extended. She then directed and then released the ball at the backboard just as the buzzer sounded.

As she landed on her feet and came back around to check, the crowd erupting in cheers informed Ruby she had been successful, and the ball had gone through the net. They had won and Ruby's teammates surrounded her, their excitement contagious. For the first time in weeks, Ruby felt a sense of accomplishment—not because they had won, but because she had faced her emotions and had successfully channeled them into something positive.

Leaving the court that night, Alex caught up with her. "You were amazing out there, Ruby. What changed?"

She smiled, the memory of Sapphire's words fresh in her mind. "I just... stopped running."

Things slowly started turning, and Ruby sensed she had rounded the corner on regaining control of her life.

Having lunch with Alex at the mall on Saturday, he took a sip of water and said, "Ruby, you've come a long way. You're so much happier these days, and I am so glad to see it."

She looked at him with a slight smile. "For a long time, I thought I had to hide everything," Ruby admitted. "Pretend I was okay. But now... I think I need to face things instead. I need to own them and then let them out."

Alex smiled, his voice warm. "That's brave, Ruby. Talking about difficult things takes a lot of courage. I guess we all have things we don't like but sharing them—that's not easy."

Ruby smiled and then explained another one of those dreams of hers to Alex, who listened patiently and attentively. She concluded the recap of her dream by saying, "The bottom line is—I think Sapphire is right... I need to face my emotions and not run away from them."

He nodded solemnly at this declaration. "Well, you know I'll help you any way that I can. I'm always here for you, Ruby."

Ruby looked deeply into his eyes. "I can't tell you how much it means to me to have your friendship and support, Alex!" She sipped from her cup of tea. "This hasn't been easy, by any means. I never even managed to work up the courage to tell Aqua anything about my dreams, and she is supposedly my best friend."

She took a bite of a french fry, and after carefully chewing and swallowing it, she continued, "I guess I'm learning that there are a lot of feelings inside that I have to face, and also parts of myself that I don't want to admit having. However, this whole process made me understand that it is normal to feel... that it is alright to be upset, or sad, or even afraid." She looked up at Alex, who was nodding contemplatively. "The point is we should not let such emotions rule our lives. We can have strength in our vulnerability, which makes us grow and heal."

Seeing Alex's bright blue eyes focused on her with a twinkle of attention as she spoke, Ruby felt proud and thankful at the same time.

As the next few weeks passed, Ruby began to reconstruct her outlook on living. She was, once again, able to concentrate on school, she hung out with friends, and she continued to restore her connections with her mom and Mia. Sapphire City was still a shadow city to her, an image removed from sunlight because an object was in the way, but now it meant sanctuary, not mayhem. She had the power to restore the light.

And yet, perhaps Ruby's greatest challenge still lay ahead. With Ms. Carter's guidance and encouragement, Ruby knew that the time had come to have a supportive, yet honest, discussion with her mom.

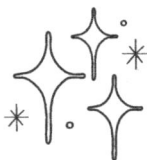

Chapter 14

Tough Conversations

One cold and windy Tuesday afternoon, Ruby stood outside the kitchen, her heart pounding as she watched her mom who sat slouched over the table, staring at a half-empty wine glass. The late-afternoon sunlight slanted through the blinds, highlighting the deep lines of exhaustion on her mom's face.

For weeks now, Ruby had thought about this moment, rehearsing what to say. But now that she was here, the words felt heavy, stuck somewhere between her chest and her throat.

Shadow meowed softly, brushing against Ruby's leg as if urging her forward. Taking a deep breath, she stepped into the kitchen.

"Mom," Ruby said quietly.

Her mother startled, her hand jerking and sloshing wine onto the table. She grabbed a napkin, dabbing at the spill with trembling hands. "Ruby, you scared me. What's wrong?"

Ruby hesitated, her fingers curling into fists at her sides. "We need to talk."

Her mother glanced at her, the tension between them almost tangible. "I'm listening."

Ruby sat down across from her, the table a fragile barrier between them. "I... I'm worried about you."

Her mom laughed, but it was hollow, forced. "Worried about me? I'm fine. I'm the one who is worried about you!"

At first, Ruby did not know how to respond, but she remained firm in her conviction. "We are not talking about me. We are talking about you."

"And I'm fine, so let's just drop the subject!"

In the silence that followed, Ruby found herself shaking her head. When she looked across the table, her mom had that twisted smile on her face that shouted out to anyone around that nothing at all was well, and this gave Ruby renewed confidence to continue.

"No, you're not," Ruby said, her voice firm. She surprised herself with how steady she sounded. "You've been drinking a lot, Mom. It's not fine. It's not okay."

Her mother's expression hardened. "Don't start with me, Ruby. Who are you to tell me what is, or what isn't, okay?" She picked up her glass of wine and with the same hand pointed a crooked finger at Ruby. "Better for you to mind your own business, if you know what's good for you."

"It is my business!" Ruby declared. "You're my mother and you're Mia's mother, but very often you do not act like a mother at all!" Ruby shot her most intense stare deeply into her mother's eyes.

Her mom took a sloppy swig of the wine. "I can't expect you to understand—"

"I do understand!" Ruby cut in, her voice rising. "I understand that you're hurting. I know you miss Dad and Liam. I miss them too, every single day. But drinking isn't going to bring them back. It's not going to make it better."

Tears welled in her mother's eyes, but she quickly blinked them away. "You think it's that simple? You think I don't know how much I've messed up? I do. I see it every time I look in the mirror. But this..." she held her wine glass high up into the air, "this is the only thing that makes the pain bearable."

Ruby's chest tightened, anger and sadness mixing into a knot of emotions. But rather than recoil, she did as Ms. Carter had advised. She reached across the table, her hand trembling as she placed it over her mom's. "I don't need you to be perfect, Mom. I just need you to try. For me. For Mia."

Her mom's lips quivered, and after another moment, a tear slipped down her cheek. "I don't know if I can."

"You can," Ruby said, her voice soft but unwavering. "We'll do it together. We'll figure it out. But you have to take the first step."

For a long moment, her mom didn't say anything. She studied the look in Ruby's eyes, the concern, the tension, and the determination. Ruby hoped her mom knew that even if not for herself, she must try for her daughters' sakes. Ruby knew her mom might not have felt ready at this very moment, but she no longer had any choice. Slowly, her mom nodded. "Okay. I'll consider giving it a try soon enough. But that is the best I can promise."

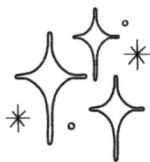

Chapter 15

Turning Point

T he first week passed in a fragile
truce. Her mom drank tea instead
of wine, though Ruby noticed her fingers tapping restless rhythms on the
mug. By day nine, Ruby found three
empty seltzer cans in the recycling —
her mom's "healthy alternative" that

still let her crack something open at five o'clock.

On day fourteen, the house smelled like lemon-scented Pledge and—burnt toast? Mia's "breakfast special" again. Ruby scraped black crumbs into the trash when something clinked under the sink. A vodka bottle, half-gone, wedged behind the bleach like it was hiding.

Not again. Or... still?

Shadow butted his head against her shin, purring too loud for the moment. She nudged him away, but he just flopped on her foot. Typical cat logic—comfort when you least want it.

The floor creaked. Mom stood in the doorway, dish towel twisted like she was wringing a neck. Their eyes met, then darted to the bottle.

"It's not—" Mom's voice cracked. "For emergencies. Like when the… the plumbing…"

Ruby's laugh came out sharp as a knife. "Emergency plumbing? That's new."

Mom grabbed the bottle. Her left hand shook—the one Dad used to hold during thunderstorms. *Funny how bodies remember what brains try to forget.*

The bottle's neck gleamed like Sapphire's smile in the lamplight. Ruby's vision doubled—for a second, the kitchen tiles cracked into glass streets, sticky with that neon-slick rain from the city. She gripped the counter. *Not now. Not here.*

Shadow sneezed. The sound made Mom jump, vodka sloshing onto her sleeve. She stared at the wet patch like it'd tell her what to do.

Ruby reached for the dishrag. "Just say it's hard."

Mom's breath hitched. "It's hard."

The words hung there, raw and ugly. Outside, a neighbor's kid shrieked about a trampoline. Normal life, moving on without them.

Mom's fingers tightened around the bottle. Then—slow as sunrise— she turned and poured the remaining vodka down the drain. The glugging sounded like a heartbeat slowing.

Ruby reached for the dishrag to clean her sleeve, but Mom caught her wrist. "No. I'll do it." Her fingers still trembled, but her voice didn't. "And I'll call that counselor tomorrow. The one from... from the hospital that time."

Shadow butted his head against Mom's ankle, his purr vibrating through the quiet. Ruby watched her mother's shoulders rise and fall, the way they used to before reading Liam his favorite bedtime story—that same measured breath.

This wasn't a promise. Not yet. But the bottle in the recycling bin made a different sound than the ones before. Emptier. Final.

Several weeks later, Ruby found herself standing just outside the community center on a cool Thursday evening. Through the wide windows, she could see a circle of folding chairs arranged beneath soft fluorescent lights. Her mom sat among them, a Styrofoam cup in hand, her back straight and her expression anxious but present.

Ruby had insisted on walking with her, even though she waited outside. She wasn't sure why—maybe just to make sure her mom went in, or maybe to witness this moment for herself.

Inside, a woman with kind eyes and a notepad smiled and said something Ruby couldn't hear, and the group shifted, murmured, settled in. Her mom nodded, cleared her throat, and slowly began to speak. Ruby couldn't make out the words, but she didn't need to. The act of showing up said enough.

Afterward, her mom stepped out, wrapping a knit cardigan around her shoulders. She looked surprised to see Ruby still waiting.

"How was it?" Ruby asked softly.

Her mom paused. "Hard. But... good."

Ruby nodded. "You're really doing it."

Her mom smiled—a small, tired, genuine smile. "One day at a time, right?"

Ruby stepped forward and gave her mom a hug, and for the first time, it felt like they were on the same side of something.

Relief washed over Ruby, but she knew this was only the beginning. "Thank you, Mom."

Her mother pulled her hand away to wipe her eyes. "I'm sorry, Ruby. For everything. For how I've treated you, for making you feel like you had to take care of Mia and me."

Ruby shook her head, tears pricking her own eyes. "I love you, Mom. We'll get through this." They remained quiet for several minutes.

Shadow jumped onto the table, his soft purring breaking the heavy silence. Ruby and her mom both laughed, the sound a tentative, fragile bridge between them. As the sunlight faded and the room grew dim, Ruby felt something she hadn't felt in a long time—*hope.*

Even though she had found renewed strength, insight, and resources, things were not always easy. Yet slowly but surely, Ruby felt motivated to heal properly once and for all from the devastation due to both past and current familial events—and only then did nightmares begin to decrease in frequency, until they almost finally stopped coming altogether.

If one did happen after that initial cessation, she became more self-aware during those times. Instead of seeing Sapphire as an enemy reminding her of her inner demons, now something entirely different took place: the blue-haired girl acted as a guide helping Ruby navigate internal struggles that might otherwise tear her soul.

Sapphire was neither friend nor foe, just another part of herself that had become separated from the rest long ago but had since been found again.

One evening while sitting alone inside the very same bedroom where darkness had once consumed everything except the darkest corners themselves, with Shadow purring so contentedly against her chest, there arose this feeling of peace that hadn't graced her heart in many years. She still knew there would be challenges ahead, however, she also understood that she wouldn't be facing them alone.

As the sun began to set, she sat by the window watching all the colors blend in a beautiful dance. She smiled, feeling peace.

The door opened and Mia walked in. "Ruby, can I sit with you?"

"Of course," she replied, patting the spot beside her in her favorite chair.

They watched the sunset together as the colors painted a promise of new beginnings across the sky. With Mia soon asleep against her side, Ruby considered that there would be obstacles on this road too, but she also knew that she was strong enough to conquer them. As the sun dipped below the horizon, she felt a deep sense of conclusion.

The turbulent emotions she had fought much of her life were now more like old friends—still present, but no longer in control. She could recognize them, comprehend them, and allow them to move on. Ruby would welcome any new obstacles in life but would now see them as a path and a roadmap to becoming even stronger.

A week later, once again watching the sun setting in a brilliant display of dazzling color, Ruby reflected on what brought her to this point. With

Shadow purring gently beside her, she thought about the journey that led her here. Her dreams of a chaotic city and confrontations with Sapphire forced her to face the darkest parts of herself. She appreciated these experiences even though they might have been terrifying at times.

Her introspection was again interrupted when someone knocked on her bedroom door. Ruby looked back and saw her mother standing in the doorframe hesitantly.

"Hi Ruby," her mom said in a low tone. "Can we talk?"

"Yes Mom, sure," Ruby answered as she carefully placed Shadow on the bed. "What's bothering you?"

Her mother walked into the room, and they sat side by side on the bed. "I've been thinking about our conversation regarding my drinking... I've been thinking about us... Mia... And I think I am ready to stop... I want to be better for my girls."

Ruby was overwhelmed by emotions; it was one thing for her to suggest to her mom that she stop drinking. But it was another to hear from her mom that her mom's hope for sobriety had settled into a decision. She reached out for her mom's hand and took it gently within hers.

"That's so great to hear, Mom," Ruby said happily, feeling a sense of accomplishment and relief. "We're going to go together through this: we will always support you."

Tears welled up in Mother's eyes while she pulled Ruby into a hug. "I love you so much, Ruby. I'm sorry for everything."

"I love you, Mom." At that moment,

Ruby breathed deeply and felt a bit more healing inside.

As they sat together, watching as light from the setting sun slowly faded away into darkness, it dawned on Ruby that their family was only beginning its journey together. They had just started and there would be a long way to go. Nonetheless, Ruby felt a bit more closure as darkness took over where the sunlight used to be; demons faced, emotions embraced, and the future found.

An uncertain tomorrow lay ahead for sure, but she was ready for it, one sunset at a time.

That night, Ruby dreamed of the cliffs.

Not the ones from Sapphire City— no glittering bridges or crumbling glass beneath her feet. These were the real cliffs. The ones by the ocean where she used to go with Dad and Liam. Only... everything was quieter now. No wind. No seagulls. Just the hush of memory pressing in from all sides.

She stood barefoot in the dew-damp grass, the horizon blurring pink and gold. The sun hadn't quite risen yet.

And then she saw him.

Liam.

He stood at the edge of the cliff, hands in the pockets of that old denim jacket he never let her borrow. His hair was longer, messier, and the corners of his mouth pulled into that familiar half-smile—half amusement, half knowing too much.

"Hey, Bird," he said.

Her breath caught.

"You're not real," she whispered.

Liam shrugged. "Maybe not. Or maybe you just needed to see me."

She didn't know whether to cry or tackle him. She took a step forward but stopped. "You left."

"I had to," he said gently. "But I never stopped being proud of you."

Ruby's chest ached. "I'm trying. But I miss you so much."

"I know," he said. "And it's okay to miss me. But you don't have to carry it all alone, Ruby. You're not the glue holding everyone together. You're just... you. And that's enough."

"I don't feel like enough."

He looked out toward the waves. "You remember the time you climbed this cliff without either of us noticing?"

She laughed quietly. "Dad freaked out."

"And you were what—nine?"

"Barely." She smiled at the memory.

"You've always been braver than you knew," he said, turning back to her. "Even when it hurts."

She didn't say anything. The lump in her throat was too thick.

He stepped forward and placed his hand over her heart. "You're doing the hard stuff. Talking. Feeling. Forgiving."

She blinked, and the cliff blurred again. He was fading.

"Don't go."

"I never really left," he said. "Not all the way."

Then his voice grew faint, like a wave retreating.

"Keep going, Ruby. You're almost there."

And she woke up—tears on her cheeks, but her chest was lighter.

Outside her window, the first light of dawn was just beginning to rise. Shadow stretched and blinked at her from the foot of the bed. Ruby lay still for a moment, hand resting over her heart where Liam's had been.

She didn't need the dream to be real.

She just needed to believe the words he said.

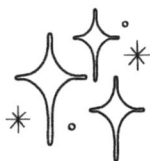

Chapter 16

Camp Counselor

Time had a way of sneaking by. And one morning, when Ruby got up, she could hear birds twittering outside her window. Another summer had arrived, and Shadow was curled up at the foot of her bed, his soft purring a familiar comfort.

This summer was different from years before when she was a teenager. Today was a special day. Ruby was about to embark on her first day as a junior camp counselor at a summer camp for troubled adolescents. It was something she had been looking forward to for years, having been motivated by her journey of healing and self-discovery.

She got dressed quickly, excitement bubbling inside her like soda bubbles. Her mother was downstairs making breakfast for them; *they had come so far in rebuilding their relationship.* Her mother had sought counseling and group support for her drinking problem during Ruby's college life, and they were closer than ever before.

"Good morning, Mom," Ruby greeted with a smile on her face as she walked into the kitchen.

"Morning Ruby," her mom said with proud eyes, "are you ready for your first day?"

"Absolutely!" replied Ruby snagging a piece of toast. "I'm mostly excited, but also kind of nervous."

"You'll be great," her mom assured. "Trust me—always remember you have so much to offer those kids."

Mia joined them at the table beaming with excitement for Ruby. "You're going to be an awesome counselor, Ruby!"

Ruby hugged Mia gratefully, saying, "Thanks Mia!"

As she left the house, Shadow meowed from the window as if wishing her luck; she smiled back and waved at him, suddenly feeling a surge of confidence within herself. *I know I can make a difference.*

At camp, Mrs. Turner, the kind-hearted camp director, introduced Ruby to other coaches and showed her around. A no-nonsense type of woman, Mrs. Turner had hired Ruby after reading what she wrote in her application form, impressed by this girl's story and seeing her potential.

"You have a unique perspective on things, Ruby," Mrs. Turner said. "You will probably get through to these children when others might not."

The summer air was thick with the smell of pine and campfires as Ruby made her way to the small activity cabin, where a group of six teenagers waited for her. The sound of their chatter and occasional bursts of laughter floated through the open door, but when Ruby stepped inside, the room fell quiet.

She had braced herself for this moment and took a deep breath as six pairs of eyes turned toward her, a mix of curiosity, skepticism, and disinterest.

"Hi, everyone," Ruby said, her voice steady despite her nerves. "I'm Ruby, and I'll be your counselor this week. I know some of you probably aren't thrilled to be here, but I promise we're going to do all we can to make this a good experience."

One boy with shaggy hair and a permanent scowl etched on his face crossed his arms. "Yeah, sure," he muttered.

Ruby smiled faintly. She understood what it was like to be uncertain of others trying to help you. "It's okay if you're not sold on this yet. I get it— I've been there. But if you're willing to give this a shot, I think we can make some progress."

A few of the teens exchanged glances, their expressions softening just a little. Ruby watched them closely and her heart lifted. It was a small step, but it was a step in the right direction, nonetheless.

Over the next few days, Ruby worked tirelessly to connect with the group. She led them in team-building activities, encouraged them to share their thoughts during reflection time, and listened carefully when they opened up, no matter how small or hesitant their confessions were.

There had been a few uncertain moments and a few holdouts, but gradually it seemed the group had decided that Ruby was there with the sole purpose of being a good influence, and that she would not be troubled by an occasional rift of dissent.

One afternoon, as they sat on the dock after a kayaking session, Ruby noticed a girl named Emily sitting apart from the others, staring out at the lake.

"Mind if I join you?" Ruby asked, sitting down beside her.

Emily shrugged but didn't say no.

Ruby looked out at the water, the sun sparkling on its surface. "This place is pretty peaceful, huh?"

Emily nodded; her arms wrapped around her knees. "It's better than home."

Ruby glanced at her, sensing the weight of the world behind the girl's words. "Home can be tough sometimes," she said softly. "I know it was for me."

Emily looked at her, curiosity flickering in her eyes. "Really? You don't seem like you'd have problems at home."

Ruby smiled briefly and nodded. "Well, believe me, I've had my share. Losing people I loved, dealing with a very sad mom, and a lot of other stuff I didn't know how to handle. It was hard."

Emily was quiet for a moment. "So, how did you get through it?"

Ruby hesitated, then said, "My dreams and nightmares were telling me what I had to do. I had been holding myself together by keeping all my emotions bottled up inside and not sharing my pain with anyone. I started by letting myself feel what I was feeling. And then I knew I had to share what I was feeling with someone I could trust would handle it okay. I went in to see my school counselor—it wasn't easy, and it didn't fix everything, but it helped me figure out how to move forward."

Emily nodded slowly, her gaze returning to the water. "Maybe I should try that."

The next few days were full of activities, counseling sessions, and intimate conversations between lost and found souls. Intuitively, Ruby found that she was able to connect with these kids at a deep level; they resonated with her experiences, and this helped them to share more about their own lives, fears, and dreams. The bonds she forged with them were strong and authentic.

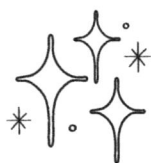

Chapter 17

Campfire Lessons

On their last night at camp, the
group gathered around a crack-
ling fire, its orange light dancing on
their faces as they laughed and remi-
nisced amongst themselves about their
favorite times at camp. The smell of
toasted marshmallows filled the air, and

the sound of crickets blended with the distant rustle of leaves.

As the conversations waned, Ruby cleared her throat. "Can I share something with you guys?"

She looked into the eyes of the campers around her, each of them filled with hope and vulnerability. She took a deep breath before beginning to speak. A bit tentatively at first, she said, "Looking back on what got me through my most difficult times, it was not easy. There were a lot of feelings I had to face and parts of myself that I did not want to admit."

The teens turned their full attention to her, their curiosity piqued. As she continued, their eyes focused on her with strict attention, and Ruby felt proud and thankful at the same time because of this. *She had come full circle by turning her anguish into a wellspring of strength and inspiration for others.*

"The process of recovery made me understand that it is normal to feel. It is alright to be upset, or sad, or even afraid. The point is we should not let such emotions rule our lives. We can have strength in our vulnerability, and this can lead to our growth and healing."

She paused and looked at each set of eyes watching her closely. "I wasn't sure I was the right person to be your counselor," Ruby went on, her voice soft but steady. "Several years ago, I went through some really hard stuff. I lost my dad and my brother, and for a long time, I didn't know how to deal with it. I was angry, sad, confused... and I felt completely alone."

A few of the teens shifted from their positions sitting around the campfire, their expressions growing more serious.

"I tried to push everything down, to pretend I was fine," Ruby continued. "But it didn't work. I was stuck until someone told me something important: *It's okay to feel. It's okay to be sad or scared or mad.* Those feelings don't make you weak—they make you human."

The fire crackled, filling the silence as the teens absorbed her words.

"Now, I'm not saying I have it all figured out," Ruby added with a small smile. "But I've learned that facing what's inside you instead of running from it is the first step to healing. And you don't have to do it alone."

For a moment, no one spoke. Then, to Ruby's surprise, the shaggy-haired boy broke the silence. "That's... actually kinda cool," he muttered, his customary scowl softening.

Emily nodded. "Yeah. Thanks for telling us. And thanks for all you've done for each of us!"

Ruby smiled, a warmth spreading through her chest. "Thanks for listening. I'm proud of all of you for being here, for trying. You're stronger than you think."

As the fire burned low and the stars emerged in the sky, the group talked late into the night, their walls slowly crumbling.

Ten years after the loss, as Ruby looked back, she realized that so many things had changed in her life. Her mother was still going for counseling sessions and participating in support groups, and their relationship continued to heal. Mia had become happier, and the house seemed lighter and more hopeful. Shadow remained a solid source of solace and company, always providing a gentle paw or sound.

Ruby watched the sun dip below the horizon and felt a deep sense of conclusion. The turbulent emotions she had fought much of her life were now more like old friends—still present, but no longer in control. She could recognize them, comprehend them, and allow them to move on.

Her grades had improved back in high school and now in college, and she found herself happy studying again. Aqua was still a good friend, but she had moved on to a college out of state and was thriving in her new life. Alex remained her loyal friend and was always there to listen or lend a shoulder to lean on. They often spoke about their dreams and future things they would do together once grown.

As she sat in her room one evening with an open notebook in front of her, she wrote an essay about personal growth and resilience using her own experiences as examples. Shadow watched her write from his cozy bed close by.

Ruby took a break as she thought about how far she had come. She had fought off the inner demons, embraced emotions, and discovered the strength that lay dormant within her spirit. Her visions of the chaotic city along with the encounters with Sapphire that had haunted her nights were tough but also marked the turning point in her life.

A smile spread across her face as she felt proud of herself for coming this far. The journey wasn't over, but she was ready for whatever came next. With Shadow by her side and family members and friends rallying behind her, she knew nothing could defeat her—not even remotely!

As she continued to write her essay, she contemplated her future: *"Years later, standing at the edge of the same cliff where she, her father, and brother used to come, Ruby was watching over the ocean as the sun set in a burst of colors. Now older and wiser, she had found peace within herself. These lessons she had learned from her dream city had remained with her as a guiding force through both good and bad times."*

She stopped again and realized how, nowadays, she always smiled while thinking about Sapphire and their journey. It had been a long and rough road but had led her to a place of understanding and peace. Shadow, who was now an old but still lively cat, rubbed against her legs reminding her that love and companionship were always there when needed.

Often Ruby thought about her family's journey together. She and her mother had been able to build back their relationship, and Mia had grown into an outgoing young woman who loved singing.

She turned away as soon as the sun sank below the horizon, ready to embrace the impending future. She had discovered herself capable of anything, along with the strength that would make it all possible.

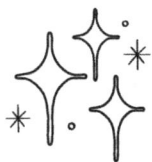

Chapter 18

Return to Sapphire City

S he did finally come back to "the city in dreams," not while sleeping but in her wakeful life. She did this purposefully by closing her eyes and meditating on her dream, placing herself back in Sapphire City, but this time taking control of its environment.

As she stood amongst the towering skyscrapers and glass streets, she wondered at the technological revolution that had once seemed like some sci-fi movie to her eyes only yesterday. The city wasn't about chaos any longer, only possibility and hope.

She visited every landmark that had featured in her dreams where everyone reminded her of the difficulties she had overcome. The city now felt so connected somehow; like it belonged among other souls inside her.

Ruby stood before an enormous screen just like the one on which Sapphire first showed her face.

Sapphire, her dream self, appeared beside her, glowing softly.

Ruby thought about everything she had faced thus far in her life. "I still don't understand why you pushed me to do all this," she said quietly.

Sapphire's voice was calm and reassuring. "It's because you've always had the strength inside you. I'm just a reflection of what you can become. You needed to face your fears and see for yourself."

Ruby took a moment to absorb her words. "I'm not sure I'm ready to let go of what's real, though."

"You don't have to," Sapphire replied. "What's real is the strength you've gained. You're not alone in this, Ruby. You carry that strength with you, always."

Ruby nodded, finally understanding. "I think I get it now. I'll be okay."

Sapphire's form flickered as if to say goodbye. "You'll always have that strength, even when I'm not here."

As sunlight disappeared over the city, Ruby felt closure. She had confronted her demons and embraced her feelings, making a way forward. The future was uncertain but one sunset at a time, she knew she could face it.

Ruby would forge ahead with Shadow by her side leaving the past behind and entering the light of a new day. There would always remain more to be accomplished, and this journey wasn't yet over. But she knew, without any doubt, that whatever followed would also come to pass since she had power and bravery within herself. It was on this note that Ruby looked forward to another sunrise in full awareness of its promises.

◆ ＊ ◆ ＊ ◆

Mia

Sometimes at night, Mia would lie still in bed and pretend she was a tree.

Trees didn't have to talk. Trees didn't flinch when voices got loud. Trees just stood and waited until the wind passed.

Her room was dark, except for the faint glow of the hallway nightlight— left on mostly for her. Shadow often came in around midnight, curling himself into a comma at her feet. She liked the weight of him, the way his purring filled the quiet.

She would trace patterns on her bedsheet with one finger, drawing the cliffs from memory—the cliff where Ruby once told her everything would be okay.

Sometimes, she wasn't sure if that had really happened or if she had just needed it to.

Mia saw more than people thought. She saw Ruby tiptoe past their mom's room, flinching at the floorboards. She saw the way Ruby gripped her pencil too tightly at the table. And she saw the way Ruby smiled differently when she talked to Alex than when she talked to Aqua.

She never said anything. Not for a long time.

But when Ruby hugged her after that bad day at school—the day Mia had been called "the girl with the broken family"—Mia had felt something shift. Like her big sister wasn't a tree either. Like they were both just people.

And maybe that was okay.

Mia rolled onto her side and looked out the window.

The moon was out. The sky was clear.

Somewhere downstairs, she heard a chair scrape quietly against the kitchen floor. Maybe their mom couldn't sleep either. Maybe no one in this house really could, not all the way.

But Shadow was still at her feet, and Ruby's door was cracked just enough for a sliver of hallway light to fall into the room.

Mia closed her eyes.

She was tired of pretending to be a tree.

◈ ✳ ◈ ✳ ◈

By the following summer, Ruby was mentoring younger girls at a youth grief camp — the kind of space she once needed but never had. She kept a journal through it all.

Years passed, quiet but not empty. Ruby grew older. So did Shadow. So did the stories she once told only to herself. She'd gone from surviving to mentoring, from being the quiet girl with bottled-up feelings to the one helping others unpack their own.

One summer afternoon, with the air just beginning to carry the promise of sunset, she returned to the place where it all began.

Week One

I don't know why I thought volunteering would feel like a movie montage. Like, I'd show up, say something vaguely wise, and someone would smile and say I helped. Instead, it's just... messy. Mostly, I listen. A lot of long silences and tapping feet and looking down.

Which feels familiar.

Sometimes I see pieces of myself in them. Not whole mirrors—more like fragments. A way someone winces at their own words. Or says "I'm fine" too fast. I don't jump in. I just nod and stay.

It's strange how that's the thing I used to fear the most. The staying.

Week Three

Today, one of the newer kids—Tanya—said she didn't think anyone noticed she was hurting. And all I could think was, "I did." But I didn't say that. I just passed her a paperclip. We made a chain of them on the table. Didn't talk much.

I think sometimes words get in the way.

Ms. Carter said I have a way of making people feel safe. That made me cry in the parking lot.

Week Five

I caught myself repeating something Sapphire once said. Not word-for-word. But the spirit of it. Something about how healing isn't a race. Just a direction.

I don't dream about her as much anymore. But sometimes I catch glimpses—in the way sunlight hits a window, or in the breath between someone's panic and their pause.

Maybe she's not gone. Just part of the air now.

Week Seven

Mia drew a picture of me with a cape. She said I look like a camp counselor superhero. I told her I think capes get in the way when you're washing dishes.

She said, "Yeah, but they look cooler when you're hugging someone."

I think that's the best review I've ever gotten.

I'm still learning how to show up for others.

But I'm starting to believe I'm not pretending anymore.

Chapter 19

A New Kind of Peace

The air at the cliff still smelled like pine needles and salt.

Ruby stood at the edge, the wind tugging at the hem of her jacket, Mia beside her, now taller and braver than she'd ever imagined. Behind them, a teenage girl with blue braids and a chipped tooth adjusted her backpack and squinted toward the ocean.

"You used to come here with them?" the girl asked, brushing hair from her eyes.

"Every summer," Ruby said softly. "It was our place."

Mia dropped to the ground and crossed her legs, pulling out a sketch-pad. "It still is."

The camper—her name was Kayla—didn't speak for a long while. She just sat there, quiet, like she was waiting for permission to breathe. Ruby remembered that feeling.

Finally, Kayla asked, "Do you really think people get better? For real?"

Ruby turned to her. "I think healing isn't about erasing what hurt you. It's about carrying it differently."

Mia added, without looking up from her sketch, "And sometimes, you don't carry it alone."

They sat in silence, the wind flattening the grass, waves colliding against the cliffs below. In the distance, a hawk cut across the sky in a long, slow arc.

Ruby closed her eyes. She could still hear her father's laugh if she tried hard enough. Liam's sneakers scraping across the rocks. She didn't feel haunted anymore.

Just whole.

Shadow's collar jingled softly as the old cat nestled between her and Mia, fur graying but purr just as strong.

Ruby smiled.

"Let's stay a little longer," she said. And they did.

$$\diamond * \diamond * \diamond$$

The years ahead would bring many changes. Ruby would graduate from college, pursue a career she loved, and travel around the world. She would forge lasting friendships and build a life full of experiences and memories. Throughout all these things, Shadow was ever present in her soul with his symbolic representative of love's endurance.

She had faced her inner darkness and had come out stronger, always ready to welcome the sunrise of another day.

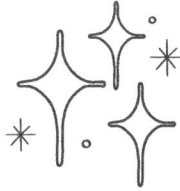

Bonus Story

The Bus Ride

A Prequel to Embracing Shadow

The Greyhound bus squealed like a rusty hinge as it pulled up to the platform, its silver body slicing through the early morning mist. Ruby stood on the balls of her feet, squinting down the road like she could hold the moment in place just by watching it closely enough.

"Dad, is this the one?" she asked.

Her father glanced at the printed ticket in his hand, then at the long silver car slowing to a stop. "This is it. The bus to Chicago, the Windy City."

Ruby's stomach clenched. She didn't like the sound of it—windy from what? A blast of air that would pull Liam away? A life where her favorite person wasn't just a shout away?

Liam adjusted the straps on his duffel bag and gave her a side glance. "You okay, Bird?"

She rolled her eyes. "Don't call me that."

"You said you wanted a nickname."

"Yeah, but not that one. I'm not a bird."

"You chirp when you're excited."

"I do not!"

Their father chuckled, running a hand through Liam's unruly hair. "Leave your sister alone."

But Ruby wasn't really mad. She liked when Liam teased her—it made her feel like things hadn't changed yet.

The bus station was quiet except for the occasional cough or shuffle of footsteps. The bus driver checked tickets a few feet away, his polo shirt too bright for the foggy morning.

Liam crouched in front of Ruby and rested his arms on his knees. "Hey, remember what we talked about? About looking after Mom?"

Ruby nodded, her eyes stinging.

"And Mia too, okay? Even if she's annoying."

"I know." Her voice came out thinner than she wanted. "But I don't want you to go."

He smiled. Not his goofy smile—the other one. The one that meant he got it. "It's just college. Not outer space. I'll call all the time."

"Promise?"

"Promise." He held out his pinky. She wrapped hers around his without hesitation.

Behind them, their dad cleared his throat. He wasn't crying, not exactly—but Ruby had seen that look before. The same one he wore at the last parent-teacher conference when he told her teacher that Ruby "felt things deeply."

Liam stood and pulled his dad into a hug, holding him tight. "Thanks for everything, Dad."

"You make me proud, kid," their father said. "Just don't let those university libraries turn you into a hermit."

Liam laughed. "No promises."

The bus driver waved. Time to board.

Ruby reached out impulsively and hugged him again, tighter than before. "Don't forget me."

"I couldn't if I tried." His voice was muffled against her hair. "I'll miss you like crazy."

And then he turned, stepping onto the bus.

She watched him find a window seat and press his hand to the glass as the bus pulled away. She raised hers in return, their palms separated by inches—and everything.

The platform grew quiet again. Just the three of them left now. Ruby, her dad, and the space Liam used to fill.

They started to walk back to the car. Her father kept one hand on her shoulder.

"You okay, Bird?"

She didn't protest the nickname this time.

She just nodded, her eyes on the road.

The bus was already gone.

But she could still feel it.

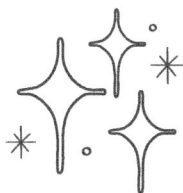

Bonus Story

The Space Between Stops

A Father's Perspective

The silence in the car after the bus pulled away was the kind that knew how to settle in your bones. Not awkward, not empty—just vast. Like something had been scooped out of the air and taken with Liam as he waved through the window.

Ruby sat in the passenger seat, her legs curled beneath her, face half-turned toward the direction the bus had gone long after it disappeared.

He didn't say anything. She didn't either.

He just drove.

On the highway, the wind curled through the open window like an old song. He kept his hands at ten and two, not because it mattered, but because it gave him something to do. Because if he let them fall into his lap, he wasn't sure he could pick them back up again.

He glanced at her out of the corner of his eye. She was staring out the window, quiet in the way kids only get when they're trying too hard to be brave.

"Waffle House?" he offered, nodding toward the exit sign.

She shook her head without looking up. "Not hungry."

He nodded once, flicked on the turn signal anyway, and kept going.

◇ ✳ ◇ ✳ ◇

That night, after Ruby and Mia were asleep and the dishes were stacked and the house was dark enough to make the kitchen feel like a secret, he stood at the counter with a glass of water he didn't drink.

He looked at the photo on the fridge—Liam, age six, holding Ruby upside down by her ankles like a captured treasure. She was shrieking with laughter. His wife had snapped the photo mid-chaos, and he'd loved it ever since. It was the kind of chaos you'd miss when it was gone.

And now a piece of it was gone.

He didn't cry, not really. He just stared until the image blurred, and then leaned forward, resting both elbows on the counter, the weight of memory pressing down like gravity turned mean.

He thought of the bus. The way Liam looked over his shoulder one last time. The hesitation. The unspoken things between fathers and sons that always seem to get lost in the space between stops.

He wanted to go back in time. Just two minutes. Long enough to say:

I'm scared too.

I don't know how to do this without your mom, and I don't always know how to do it with her.

I'm proud of you but also scared to death of what the world might do to you.

But the bus was already gone.

He turned off the kitchen light. The house exhaled.

In the hallway, he passed by Ruby's open door. She was curled into herself, blanket pushed down to her knees, Shadow pressed against her ribs like a comma. She looked so small in the half-light, like something precious the world hadn't figured out how to protect yet.

He stood there longer than he should've. Thinking about responsibility. About how loving your kids was only half the job. The other half was being brave enough to let them go, and strong enough to stay behind.

He reached in and gently pulled the blanket over her shoulders. She didn't stir.

"Goodnight, Bird," he whispered. His voice cracked on the word.

He closed the door softly behind him.

And went back to the bedroom, where the bus hadn't stopped—but grief was already on the road ahead of it.

Acknowledgments

This story began as a piece of creative writing homework — the spark of imagination that transformed into an entire world. *Embracing Shadows* wouldn't exist without the people who inspired me to transform that spark into the book you currently have in your hands.

To my family – your unwavering support during my creative writing process reinforced my resolve to move this story past the rigid boundaries of the classroom. I cherish your support of my love for storytelling since the very beginning.

To my friends – I thank you for the daily musings of life that you have shared with me. As my friends, you have walked with me through the paths of life and imagination. I appreciate the cheer, creative aid, and empathy you offer every day.

To my teachers – I owe you a thank you for all the support I have received in my creative pursuits, and for guiding me to be insightful in the way I present and translate concepts into bite-sized pieces that are easy to digest.

To my editor – I appreciate your attention to every detail. Your deep understanding of the story and your work in shaping Ruby's journey gave life to her story. Transforming jagged edges into a moment that glows takes insightful hands, and I appreciate every moment spent shaping the story with you.

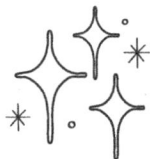

About the author

Alina V. Shi, born and raised in Vancouver, Canada, began creative writing at thirteen and published her first novel, Embracing Shadow: Ruby's Journey, at sixteen. She enjoys writing across fantasy, horror, and science fiction. Beyond writing, she is a painter, tennis player, and youth advocate, and she co-founded the Sunshine Charity, a youth-led nonprofit supporting children through creative and educational projects.

Thank you for reading
Embracing Shadow!

If you'd like to stay connected, visit
http://www.alinavshi.wordpress.com
or follow me on Instagram *@avlivq*

I'd love to share what comes next.

www.alinavshi.wordpress.com

@avlivq

Made in United States
Cleveland, OH
31 August 2025